B Beyoncé
Beyoncé

BEYONCÉ

BEYONCÉ

the QUEEN *of* POP

HEATHER E. SCHWARTZ

LERNER PUBLICATIONS ◆ MINNEAPOLIS

Lerner Publications Company
A division of Lerner Publishing Group, Inc.
241 First Avenue North
Minneapolis, MN USA 55401

For reading levels and more information, look up this title at www.lernerbooks.com.

The images in this book are used with the permission of: Monica Schipper/FilmMagic/Getty Images, p. 2; Ilya S. Savenok/Getty Images, p. 6; Ezra Shaw/Getty Images, p. 8; KMazur/WireImage/Getty Images, p. 10; Paul Howell/Liaison/Getty Images, p. 11; Jim Smeal/WireImage/Getty Images, p. 13; Martin Philbey/Redferns/Getty Images, p. 15; Everett Collection, Inc./Alamy Stock Photo, p. 16; Photo 12/Alamy Stock Photo, p. 18; Ray Amati/Getty Images, p. 19; Jeff Kravitz/FilmMagic/Getty Images, pp. 20, 34; Frank Micelotta/Getty Images, p. 22; Collection Christophel/Alamy Stock Photo, p. 25; Splash News/Alamy Stock Photo, p. 26; Rick Diamond/WireImage/Getty Images, p. 27; Entertainment Pictures/Alamy Stock Photo, p. 29; Michael Caulfield/WireImage/Getty Images, p. 30; Gregg DeGuire/FilmMagic/Getty Images, p. 32; Alo Ceballos/GC Images/Getty Images, p. 33; Kevin Mazur/Getty Images, p. 37; Kevin Mazur/WireImage/Getty Images, pp. 38, 39.

Front cover: Larry Busacca/Getty Images.

Main body text set in Rotis Serif Std 55 Regular.
Typeface provided by Adobe Systems.

Library of Congress Cataloging-in-Publication Data

The Cataloging-in-Publication Data for *Beyoncé: The Queen of Pop* is on file at the Library of Congress.
978-1-5415-2444-6 (lib. bdg.)
978-1-5415-2448-4 (eb pdf)

Manufactured in the United States of America
1-44524-34774-4/3/2018

CONTENTS

Beyoncé poses for the camera at a 2015 event in New York City's Brooklyn borough.

et to perform the Super Bowl 50 halftime show, Beyoncé Giselle Knowles planned to give fans a performance they would remember forever. It was 2016, and Americans had serious concerns about serious issues, including racism, empowerment of marginalized groups, and police brutality.

Beyoncé wasn't the headliner that night. She and Bruno Mars were guests of the main act, Coldplay. But Beyoncé was more than an entertainer. She was an artist, and she was a powerful force. If she wanted to send a message about the serious issues of the day, she could. And she did.

When Beyoncé took her turn onstage, she belted out her new song, "Formation," using her moment to pay tribute to influential African Americans before her: the King of Pop, Michael Jackson; civil rights activist Malcolm X; and the controversial Black Panthers political party, formed in 1966. Her performance rocked the stadium and showed she supported Black Lives Matter, a movement founded in 2013 to fight racism in America.

Many fans were excited to see a strong woman use

Beyoncé appears onstage with Bruno Mars during the Super Bowl 50 halftime show.

her platform to stand up for black Americans. But not everyone felt that way. The former mayor of New York, Rudy Giuliani, called Beyoncé's show a disrespectful attack on police. He said her politics didn't belong at the Super Bowl.

Beyoncé may not have liked the criticism, but she didn't back down. She didn't have to. She'd worked hard all her life to earn a place on the stage and win over millions of fans. She was ready to use her position to do more than entertain.

After the show, Beyoncé said she was proud of her Super Bowl 50 performance. It proved how far she'd come in her life and career. No matter what people thought of her, she knew she'd worked hard to reach her goals. Her efforts were paying off, and sometimes even she had a hard time believing what she'd accomplished.

"I worked so hard during my childhood to meet this goal. By the time I was 30 years old, I could do what I want," Beyoncé has explained. "I've reached that. I feel very fortunate to be in that position. But I've sacrificed a lot of things, and I've worked harder than probably anyone I know, at least in the music industry. So I just have to remind myself that I deserve it."

Baby Bey Grows Up

Beyoncé was born on September 4, 1981, in Houston, Texas. Almost from birth, she was singing, dancing, and preparing for a life on the stage and screen. Her dance teacher was the first person to notice Beyoncé's star potential and encouraged her to enter her school's talent show. At the age of seven, Beyoncé won the show, singing John Lennon's "Imagine." Beyoncé kept on singing, and at just eight years old, she was audition-ready. She tried out for and won a spot in a new group called Girl's Tyme.

By the early 1990s, Girl's Tyme had polished their act. They got the chance to go on *Star Search*, a television show that featured up-and-coming performers competing against one another. It looked as if Beyoncé was about to get her big break before she was even a teenager. "In my mind, we would perform on *Star Search*, we would win, we would get a record deal, and that was my dream at the time. There's no way in the world I would have ever imagined losing as a possibility," Beyoncé recalled years later.

Girl's Tyme worked hard to create a winning performance. They went onstage and gave it everything they had. And . . . they lost. Beyoncé was shocked. It was hard for her to understand how something like this could happen. But that early loss was far from the end of Beyoncé's career. It was only the beginning.

Beyoncé attended the High School for the Performing and Visual Arts in Houston and continued singing and dancing with Girl's Tyme. Over time, the band evolved. It was renamed Something Fresh,

A young Beyoncé poses with her sister Solange, who also showed musical talent from an early age and is a successful recording artist.

This image taken in 1993 gives a peek inside an English classroom at Beyoncé's alma mater, the High School for the Performing and Visual Arts.

Cliché, the Dolls, and Destiny. It included different lineups but always featured the rising star of the group, Beyoncé. Beyoncé's father, Mathew Knowles, left his job in sales to manage the band and run their rehearsals. He even studied artist management at a local college to learn how to do it. Beyoncé's mother, Tina Knowles, owned a hair salon where the girls practiced by performing for customers. She also sewed their costumes.

The band got better and better and scored gigs as an opening act for bigger bands, like SWV, Dru Hill, and Immature. In 1995 it seemed as if all of their hard work was about to pay off. They signed a deal to make an album with Elektra Records. It was an exciting development, but Beyoncé and her bandmates barely had time to celebrate. Before they could release an album, the company decided the girls were too young and dropped the band.

Being dropped by Elektra was a huge disappointment for Beyoncé and her bandmates. They'd been sure that signing with Elektra meant they'd made it. But like the loss on *Star Search*, they didn't let the setback get them down for long. They stuck together as a band and kept on working on their craft. They knew rejection didn't mean they weren't good. Soon others started noticing the polish and professionalism of the band as well. The missed opportunity proved to be just a minor setback.

Giving It Her All

Beyoncé worked throughout her childhood to make it as a professional performer. She didn't relax and hang out with friends on weekends and after school, as many other kids did. Instead, she rehearsed songs and dance moves and performed with her band. Devoting herself to her craft eventually led her to superstardom. But she now recognizes the sacrifices she made. "Socially I did miss out. I left school at 14 and had a tutor. I was never exposed to people long enough to make friends so my family became my friends," she has said.

Destined for Success

By 1996 the group once known as Girl's Tyme was called Destiny's Child. The name was inspired by a biblical passage. Destiny's Child included Beyoncé plus three other singers who'd also been part of Girl's Tyme: Kelly Rowland, LaTavia Roberson, and LeToya Luckett. The teens were stars in the making, ready to take on the world with their blend of pop and R & B songs.

LeToya Luckett, LaTavia Roberson, Kelly Rowland, and Beyoncé were a very close-knit quartet.

In 1997 Destiny's Child signed with Columbia Records. They worked with a team of producers, sound mixers, and other music professionals to get their sound just right. But the label gave the band a lot of creative freedom too. When they released their self-titled debut album in 1998, Beyoncé was credited as a composer as well as a vocalist.

"The label didn't really believe we were pop stars. They underestimated us, and because of that, they allowed us to write our own songs and write our own video treatments," Beyoncé said later. "It ended up being the best thing, because that's when I became an artist and took control."

Maybe some people didn't have faith that Destiny's Child would make it. But Beyoncé believed in her band and worked to make others believe in the group too. The singers' debut album launched the hit single "No, No, No" and the memorable "With Me." A year later, their second album, *The Writing's on the Wall*, was nominated for six Grammys and launched the band's first No. 1 single, "Bills, Bills, Bills."

As Destiny's Child proved their chops in the music industry, Beyoncé took the spotlight more and more. Her vocals led their songs. She stood out in their music videos. The band was evolving in a new direction, toward showcasing Beyoncé's talents and making her a star. But the band still felt like a group effort. The other singers supported Beyoncé, and she supported them too.

Yet tensions were building within the band for other reasons. LaTavia and LeToya had concerns about the

Kelly Rowland, Beyoncé, and Michelle Williams perform for fans at an appearance in Australia.

band's manager, Mathew Knowles. The singers didn't like the way he handled their money. The feud erupted into a lawsuit filed by the girls, who were still teenagers at the time, as well as a new lineup for the band. Two new singers, Michelle Williams and Farrah Franklin, replaced LaTavia and LeToya.

Destiny's Child remained a quartet for just five months before Farrah was fired. She didn't make the group's flight for a tour in Australia, where Beyoncé, Kelly, and Michelle promoted the band through radio, television, and music store appearances. Farrah argued she was sick. Mathew Knowles claimed she wasn't prepared for the hard work of being a part of Destiny's Child. Beyoncé backed him up, telling the media she wished Farrah the best, but her firing "wasn't a management decision, it was a group decision."

Mathew Knowles prepared to search for a replacement singer. But Beyoncé was proud of the work Destiny's Child did as a trio. Soon they hit the road touring with Christina Aguilera. Within a month, it was decided that Destiny's Child would remain a trio. And the three members wanted to put the drama behind them. "There's nothing but positive things going on in Destiny's Child now," Beyoncé said. "We're here to stay."

The new lineup worked hard to create a breakout third album. They spent hours in the studio writing songs and bonding over favorite snacks to fuel their long writing

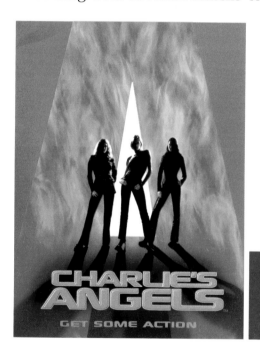

sessions. Beyoncé wrote "Independent Women, Pt. 1," which was released early for the *Charlie's Angels* movie soundtrack. It reached No. 1 on the US singles chart and stayed there so long it earned a place in *Guinness World Records*.

Charlie's Angels was a reboot of a TV series of the same name that ran from 1976 to 1981.

Taking Control

Beyoncé's father helped build her career, but when the singer turned eighteen, she started acting on her own ideas. "It took awhile for me and my dad to have an understanding," she said. "We would fight sometimes, and it took about two years, to when I was twenty, for him to realize, 'Oh, she is an adult now, and if she doesn't wanna do something, I can't make her do it.'"

Clearly, Destiny's Child had star power and a huge fan base. Some fans focused mainly on Beyoncé. Yet as her fame grew, Beyoncé considered her bandmates integral. She drew strength and support from knowing she had her sister singers by her side.

Triple Threat

After Destiny's Child released their third album, Beyoncé did some solo projects. By then the world knew her as a talented singer and dancer. In 2001 she showed that she was an actor too. Cast in *Carmen: A Hip Hopera*, she played a lead role that had her rapping for the camera. The film was a made-for-television MTV production. The following year, she moved to the big screen in the feature film *Austin Powers in Goldmember*, starring Mike Myers.

Meanwhile, Beyoncé was also working on her first solo album. Breaking out on her own was exciting. It was also scary to pursue her own dreams without her Destiny's Child bandmates.

"I already know that when I get nervous, I forget and blank out completely," she said. "That's the advantage of being in a group—where one person is weak, the other is strong."

Despite her fears, Beyoncé pressed on to produce the album, called *Dangerously in Love*. It featured other famous singers too, including Missy Elliott, Luther Vandross, and Jay-Z. Executives at Columbia Records were worried when the album was released. "They told me I didn't have one single on my album," she said later. "I guess they were kind of right. I had five."

One single that stood out even among the album's other singles was "Crazy in Love." It got especially

Beyoncé appears in character with Mike Myers in *Austin Powers in Goldmember.*

heavy radio play and had fans around the world singing along to the lyrics about all-consuming romance.

And it seemed Beyoncé wasn't just performing when it came to the feelings expressed in the song. She and Jay-Z had been dating for a couple of years and were now starting to be more open about it. He played her romantic interest in the "Crazy in Love" video, and the couple sang the song together live at the MTV Video Music Awards.

Beyonce and rapper Jay-Z sit courtside at the New York Knicks vs. Cleveland Cavaliers game at Madison Square Garden on April 14, 2004.

Beyoncé made a splash in a different way at the 2004 Grammy Awards. She took to the stage for a performance that truly showcased her skills as a solo act. In her first act of the night, she shared the stage with Prince. She impressed the legendary singer with her musical knowledge during rehearsals. Then, during the show, the duo put on an act that included a selection of Prince songs as well as Beyoncé's "Crazy in Love."

Later, she performed her song "Dangerously in Love 2," singing her solo amid dramatic props including a giant picture frame that stretched around Beyoncé. Her vocals were polished, and her act was elaborately choreographed— even ending with a dove flying onto the stage and landing on Beyoncé's hand. It left little doubt in anyone's mind that Beyoncé could be a solo star.

And that wasn't Beyoncé's only win at the awards show. She also took home five Grammys, including best R & B album. With her wins, she tied Alicia Keys, Norah Jones, and Lauryn Hill for most Grammys won by a female artist.

Beyoncé holds her five Grammys at the 2004 awards show—a clear sign that her career was taking off!

Beyoncé's first solo album was clearly a success. "I just wanted people to really hear me, hear my voice and my tastes. For the first time, I wasn't afraid, I didn't feel limited," she said. "I wanted people to hear my range, because I can sing like a rapper, I can flow, I can sing soul songs, I can do rock, and I wanted people to hear that."

Creating on Canvas

While filming *Goldmember*, Beyoncé tried yet another creative pursuit: painting. She bought some oil paints and a canvas and turned on jazz music to listen to as she worked. A few of her favorite jazz artists include Miles Davis, Shuggie Otis, and Aretha Franklin. Her first painting looked as if it might have been inspired by her look in the movie. It was an abstract picture of a woman with an Afro, just as her character has in the film.

Destiny Fulfilled

In 2004 Beyoncé turned her focus back to Destiny's Child. She was excited to continue collaborating with her bandmates. By this time, she had plenty of opportunities to keep on shining as a solo act. Companies wanted her to represent their brands, and she became the face of makeup corporation L'Oreal. She had her own perfume, True Star, on the market too. She was also set to act in the movie *The Pink Panther* with comedian and actor Steve Martin.

Yet Beyoncé didn't want to leave her bandmates behind. "This is having fun with my best friends," she said. "There is nothing sweeter than three-part harmony."

Destiny's Child dominates the stage on the Destiny Fulfilled . . . and Lovin' It tour.

Destiny's Child got to work recording *Destiny Fulfilled*. They also launched a world tour they called Destiny Fulfilled . . . and Lovin' It. They put everything they had into promoting their album and tour. The singers were truly committed to the work they were doing together–yet fans soon learned there was a bigger meaning to the name "Destiny Fulfilled." It meant the singers felt they'd done everything they'd set out to do as a band. In June 2005, they made an announcement onstage in Barcelona: The band was breaking up. Each artist planned to pursue a solo career.

For Beyoncé, that meant pursuing all kinds of creative endeavors. She'd proven herself as a singer, dancer, and actor, but she wanted to achieve even more. In January 2005, she announced the launch of her fashion line, House of Dereon. She named it after her grandmother, Agnes Dereon, and designed the collection with her mother.

Beyoncé's popularity and fame grew with everything she did, but her work wasn't just about making her own name more visible. She also wanted to serve others. In June 2005, she auctioned off about twenty of her costumes to help the VH1 Save the Music Foundation. The organization supports music programs in public schools. After Hurricane Katrina hit the Gulf Coast of the United States in August, Beyoncé, along with her family and Kelly Rowland, formed the Survivor Foundation to help provide housing for victims in the Houston area. And in November, Beyoncé was an ambassador for World Children's Day, a UNICEF event dedicated to children's empowerment.

Grace under Pressure

At the 2005 Academy Awards, Beyoncé performed three songs in front of the live audience as well as more than forty million TV viewers. Before singing "Learn to Be Lonely" from *The Phantom of the Opera*, she changed into a new dress and had her hair and makeup done with only seconds to spare. Racing to the stage, she realized her ear monitor was off and she worried she'd mess up the words to the song. Then her shoe fell off and got stuck in her long gown as she stepped down the stairs. Through it all, no one ever knew. She kept on with the show and never let on that things weren't going as she'd planned.

Class Act

As Beyoncé got involved in more and more projects, her name began appearing more and more in print and online. Articles about her often described her as quiet, humble, shy, and classy. She was known for responding in a soft-spoken way even when the media reported rumors about her.

When Beyoncé took on her first major project after leaving Destiny's Child, media rumors surfaced about Beyoncé's work style. The project was a role in the film *Dreamgirls*—about a trio of soul singers who find success on the pop charts—and some media sources speculated that Beyoncé wanted a bigger role than she had gotten. They suggested that since she was used to the spotlight, she may not be comfortable taking on work in which she wasn't the biggest star.

Beyoncé calmly quashed the rumors and shared her perspective on them. "I didn't have the part with the most drama," she said. "I was fine with that. I'm not doing this to become a star or prove that I can sing. . . . I did this mainly to know I can act, to know myself and show everyone else that I could. I'm extremely happy with the movie."

Beyoncé (*center*) played an early 1960s soul singer in the 2006 film *Dreamgirls*.

Beyoncé also kept her focus on her work instead of on what the media was saying. She got to work recording her second solo album, *B'Day*—though Beyoncé herself didn't seem to consider it work. She later said of the album that it "came . . . effortlessly." In addition, she made eight videos for a video-album version of *B'Day* (an album recorded on DVD that featured songs from *B'Day* and accompanying music videos). The recording schedule required lots of hard work and long hours, but Beyoncé said the pressure didn't bother her.

"I don't mind pressure," she said. "I'm very good under pressure. But I wanna put myself under pressure, not be pressured by someone else, or else I'm angry and it blocks my creativity." For that reason, she didn't tell many people that she was recording *B'Day*. Only those with a hands-on role in making the album knew about the project.

The release of *B'Day* came as a surprise to many people. Here Beyoncé celebrates the release of her new album in a Macy's store.

Beyoncé dons a shimmery dress at an event promoting *B'Day*.

The biggest single from *B'Day* was the song "Irreplaceable." The media speculated it was about her longtime boyfriend, rapper Jay-Z. The story line in the song had Beyoncé breaking up with her boyfriend. Fans loved it for helping them through their own breakups, and it stayed at No. 1 on the Billboard Hot 100 list for ten weeks straight.

After the release of *B'Day*, Beyoncé set off on a tour. The Beyoncé Experience tour made appearances on stages around the world throughout 2007, and it mostly went off as planned. However, there were some snags. At one concert, two fans suffered minor injuries when some of the show's fireworks spilled into the audience. Beyoncé went to see the fans in the hospital. At another show, Beyoncé lost her footing and slid down the stairs onstage. She immediately jumped up to continue the performance. She sang her next number seated on a stool, jokingly asking her audience not to post clips of her fall on YouTube.

Playing the Part

In April 2008, Beyoncé had a major moment in her personal life. She married Jay-Z—showing that not only were the breakup rumors about her and Jay-Z false, but their relationship was stronger than ever. The couple was very private about their wedding, held at the groom's penthouse in Manhattan. Only forty guests were invited. Beyoncé wore a strapless white gown designed by her mom. Jay-Z was in a black tuxedo. Neither of them performed. They were there to celebrate their love with close friends and family.

The day after their wedding, Jay-Z left on tour. Beyoncé had plenty of work to do too. She had a role in the movie *Cadillac Records,* playing iconic singer Etta James. She was also hard at work on a third album, *I Am . . . Sasha Fierce.* The title referenced her alter ego. Despite her string of successes, Beyoncé wasn't always confident and comfortable as a solo artist. She dealt with this by playing the role of Sasha Fierce, a fearless performer. Beyoncé said her cousin Angie gave Sasha her name.

As Sasha, Beyoncé felt freer to express herself onstage. She said she often lost herself when performing as Sasha and even did things she didn't remember. For example, she once threw an expensive bracelet into the crowd and had to have her cousin Angie get it back for her.

"It's kind of like doing a movie. When you put on the wig and put on the clothes, you walk different," she said.

"It's no different from anyone else. I feel like we all kind of have that thing that takes over."

I Am . . . Sasha Fierce was released in November 2008. The album sold more than four hundred thousand copies in less than two weeks. It went on to win a Grammy for Best Contemporary R & B album.

In January 2009, Beyoncé serenaded President Barack Obama and First Lady Michelle Obama during their first dance at the inaugural ball. She sang "At Last," the song made famous by Etta James in the 1960s. Two months later, she hit the road on tour.

Beyoncé plays pool in character as Etta James in the 2008 film *Cadillac Records*.

By then Beyoncé was an established superstar. She had nothing to prove and no reason to doubt herself. But still she wanted to do her best at all times. "Like everyone else, you work really hard and you want it to be great; you want your friends to like it," she said. "What makes me feel comfortable is practice and knowing I'm prepared.

But I still, of course, get nervous."

At the 2010 Grammy Awards, Beyoncé's hard work paid off. She was nominated for ten awards and won six, including her Grammy for Best Contemporary R & B Album. It was the most trophies ever won in a single Grammy night by a female artist. Thanking her fans and her husband, she called it an amazing night.

Beyoncé performs onstage at the Staples Center for the 2010 Grammy Awards in Los Angeles.

Sharing the Stage

Beyoncé found herself in a surprising spot when Taylor Swift won an award for Best Female Video at the 2009 MTV Video Music Awards. As Swift was giving her acceptance speech, Kanye West jumped up and took the microphone away from her. He told the crowd Beyoncé should have won instead.

Later that night, Beyoncé won a Video of the Year award. She graciously brought Swift onstage with her and invited her to deliver her speech.

Working Mother

Around the time of the 2010 Grammys, Beyoncé announced she was ready to let go of Sasha Fierce. She said she no longer needed her alter ego to help her let loose when she performed. Another major change in her life was also on the horizon. At the 2011 MTV Video Music Awards, Beyoncé performed the song "Love on Top." When it was over, she unbuttoned her jacket, rubbed her belly, and shared that she was pregnant. It was the biggest news of the night.

Beyoncé took some time away from work during her pregnancy. But she still had to talk to the media about all the rumors going around. She spoke out to

News of Beyoncé's pregnancy made a big splash at the 2011 VMAs!

tell fans there was no truth to talk that her pregnancy was a fake. She also halted rumors that she was snacking on unusual combinations of foods—like hot sauce, pickles, and bananas, as one story reportedly claimed!

In January 2012, Blue Ivy Carter was born. Beyoncé called her new daughter "my favorite thing in the world." She said that she could stare at Blue Ivy all day and that "my No. 1 job is to protect her."

Yet Beyoncé also remained passionate about her music career. She had a recent album out—titled 4—and between April 2013 and March 2014, she traveled the world on the Mrs. Carter Show World Tour. (Carter is Beyoncé's married name, as Jay-Z's given name is Shawn Carter.) Then, between June and September 2014, Beyoncé and Jay-Z toured together. And in the middle of the touring, Beyoncé had a surprise for fans—she was releasing yet another album, titled *Beyoncé*. Each song on the album had an accompanying video, and both the songs and videos were available for purchase exclusively online.

On the decision to release videos with each song, Beyoncé said, "I see music. It's more than just what I hear. When I'm connected to something, I immediately see a visual or a series of images that are tied to a feeling or an emotion, a memory from my childhood, thoughts about life . . . or my fantasies. And they're all connected to the music."

At the 2014 MTV Video Music Awards, Beyoncé performed songs from her self-titled album. She also landed the Michael Jackson Video Vanguard Award, which Jay-Z and Blue Ivy handed to her in front of a cheering crowd.

Beyoncé holds tight to Blue Ivy on November 4, 2014, in New York City.

It was a proud moment for Beyoncé when Jay-Z and Blue Ivy presented her with a Michael Jackson Video Vanguard Award at the 2014 VMAs.

The following year was also packed with performances and appearances for Beyoncé. She sang at the Grammys in February 2015 and collected more awards, including Best R & B Song and Best R & B Performance for her song "Drunk in Love," featuring Jay-Z. She showed up at the Met Gala—a fund-raising event for New York's Metropolitan Museum of Art—in May wearing a sparkling gossamer dress that stole the show. In September she headlined at the Made in America Festival, a Labor Day weekend concert featuring multiple performers, and sang solo works as well as songs from her Destiny's Child days.

Beyoncé was busy, but she prioritized making time for her family. In April 2015, she and Jay-Z celebrated their seventh wedding anniversary with a vacation to Hawaii. In June they took Blue Ivy along on a vacation to the Hamptons.

"I have a lot of awards. . . . I worked harder than probably anyone I know to get those things," Beyoncé said. "But nothing feels like my child saying, 'Mommy.' Nothing feels like when I look at my husband in the eyes. Nothing feels like [when] I'm respected, when I get on the stage and see I'm changing people's lives. Those are the things that matter."

Using Her Power

As a wealthy and famous performer, Beyoncé knows she has the power to help many people. In 2013 she founded BeyGood, a charity organization, during her Mrs. Carter world tour. She helped millions of people in need of shelter, employment, and other necessities around the globe.

"I now know that, yes, I am powerful. I'm more powerful than my mind can even digest and understand," she said.

Future Focus

In April 2016, Beyoncé released her sixth album, *Lemonade.* Packed with songs focused on troubled relationships, the album sparked rumors of problems in her own marriage. But Beyoncé didn't comment, preferring as usual to focus on her work instead of on media controversy. Immediately after the album's release, Beyoncé set off on her Formation World Tour with concerts throughout North America and Europe.

In February 2017, she used Instagram to announce some exciting news. She was pregnant again—this time with twins! She posted a photo of her belly along with an announcement that not one but two new babies would be joining her and Jay-Z's family.

Rumi, a girl, and Sir, a boy, were born June 13, 2017. Only about two weeks later, Jay-Z released his album *4:44*, which, like *Lemonade*, focused on relationship issues. Later that year, Jay-Z told the media that the couple had indeed gone through some difficult times. But he also said they were back on track. Beyoncé's family was secure.

Her career was rock-solid too. And it was offering her more opportunities to showcase her talents and support charitable causes. After having the twins, Beyoncé headlined a benefit concert at New York City's Barclays Center to raise funds for victims of Hurricane Harvey and Hurricane Irma. She also lent her song "Freedom" to a

Beyoncé attends the 66th NBA All-Star Game on February 19, 2017, in New Orleans, Louisiana.

documentary about issues facing girls around the world, such as child marriage, access to education, and violence.

In 2017 Beyoncé was the highest-paid woman in music, earning $105 million. She is an ever-rising star, grounded

Beyoncé offers her fans a big smile during the Formation World Tour in Santa Clara, California.

by her family as she continues reaching fans throughout the world with her art.

Being a celebrity hasn't always been easy for Beyoncé, between giving up her privacy and spending long hours perfecting her performances from the time she was a child. She knows she's sacrificed a lot. But the life she's chosen is the life she loves, and even with all of her success, she knows her family is what matters most.

Beyoncé appears in a dramatic, glittery ensemble in this image from September 2016.

"You can't put your finger on who I am. I can't put my finger on who I am. I am complicated. . . . I've been through a lot, just like everyone else," she said. "My escape was always music, and I'm so lucky that that's my job. But if I accomplished all of these things and had no one to share it with, it would be worth nothing."

IMPORTANT DATES

1981   Beyoncé Giselle Knowles is born on September 4 in Houston, Texas.

1996   Her childhood singing group, Girl's Tyme, has morphed into Destiny's Child—the group that would launch Beyoncé's career.

2001   She acts in *Carmen: A Hip Hopera*.

2003   She releases her first solo album, *Dangerously in Love*.

2004   She performs at the Grammys and wins five awards.

2005   She launches her fashion line, House of Dereon.

2006   She releases *B'Day*, her second solo album.

2007   She launches the Beyoncé Experience world tour.

2008   She marries rapper Jay-Z.

2009   She sings for President Barack Obama and First Lady Michelle Obama.

2010	She wins six Grammy Awards.
2012	Blue Ivy Carter, Beyoncé's first child, is born.
2013	Beyoncé founds her BeyGood charity organization.
2016	She releases *Lemonade*.
2017	Rumi and Sir Carter, Beyoncé's twins, are born.

SOURCE NOTES

9 Bruna Nessif, "Beyoncé's *GQ* Interview: Sexy Superstar Dishes on Super Bowl, Sacrifice, and Feeling 'Lost,'" *E! News*, January 10, 2013, http://www.eonline.com/fr/news/377260 /beyonce-s-gq-interview-sexy-superstar-dishes-on-super-bowl -sacrifice-and-feeling-lost.

10 Nick Catucci, "Watch: Beyoncé Talks about Childhood and Crushed Dreams in New Video," *Entertainment Weekly*, December 18, 2013, http://ew.com/article/2013/12/18/beyonce -feminism-self-titled-video/.

12 "Beyoncé Going Back to School?," *Lee Bailey's Electronic Urban Report*, April 19, 2012, http://www. eurweb.com/2012/04 /beyonce-going-back-to-school/.

14 Tamar Gottesman, "Exclusive: Beyoncé Wants to Change the Conversation," *Elle*, April 4, 2016, http://www.elle.com/fashion /a35286/beyonce-elle-cover-photos/.

16 Eric Schumacher Rasmussen, "Destiny's Child Manager: Member Couldn't Handle Schedule," *MTV News*, July 26, 2000, http://www.mtv.com/news/1122470/destinys-child-manager -fired-member-couldnt-handle-schedule/.

16 Teri vanHorn, "Destiny's Child Members Say They're Now a Trio," *MTV News*, August 24, 2000, http://www.mtv.com /news/1123406/destinys-child-members-say-theyre-now-a-trio/.

17 Corey Moss, "Want to Wake Up with Beyoncé? Revealing Photo Spread Takes You inside Her Morning," *MTV News*, July 12, 2006, http://www.mtv.com/news/1536180/want-to-wake-up -with-beyonce-revealing-photo-spread-takes-you-inside-her -morning/.

18 Mimi Valdés, "Beyoncé 'The Metamorphosis' (October 2002)," *Vibe*, June 28, 2011, https://www.vibe.com/2011/06/beyonce -metamophosis-october-2002/.

18 Erika Ramirez, "Beyoncé, 'Dangerously in Love': Classic Track-by-Track Review," *Billboard*, June 22, 2013, http://www .billboard.com/articles/columns/the-juice/1568019/beyonce -dangerously-in-love-classic-track-by-track-review.

20 Lisa Robinson, "Above and Beyoncé," *Vanity Fair*, November 2005, https://www.vanityfair.com/culture/2005/11/beyonce -knowles-profile-music-career.

21 Lola Ogunnaike, "Beyoncé's Second Date with Destiny's Child," *New York Times*, November 14, 2004, http://www.nytimes .com/2004/11/14/arts/music/beyonces-second-date-with-destinys -child.html.

25 Shaheem Reid, "Beyoncé Wants End to Drama over New Drama 'Dreamgirls'; Sets Tour," *MTV News*, December 12, 2006, http://www.mtv.com/news/1547863/beyonce-wants-end-to -drama-over-new-drama-dreamgirls-sets-tour/.

26 Kelefa Sanneh, "Beyoncé Bounces Back: Film, Album and Warning," *New York Times*, November 23, 2006, http://www .nytimes.com/2006/11/23/arts/music/23sann.html.

26 Moss, "Want to Wake Up with Beyoncé?"

28–29 "Beyoncé Is Sasha Fierce," *Oprah.com*, November 13, 2008, http://www.oprah.com/oprahshow/beyonces-alter-ego/all.

30 Lacey Rose, "Inside Beyoncé's Entertainment Empire," *Forbes*, June 4, 2009, https://www.forbes.com/forbes/2009/0622 /celebrity-09-jay-z-sasha-fierce-inside-beyonce-empire .html#4ac5bd9d2f68.

32 "From the Archive: Beyoncé on Giving Birth to Blue Ivy and Her Post-Pregnancy Body," *People*, February 1, 2017, http://people .com/archive/from-the-archive-beyonce-on-giving-birth-to-blue -ivy-and-her-post-pregnancy-body/.

33 Eric R. Danton, "Beyoncé Surprises with New Album Release," *Rolling Stone*, December 13, 2013, http://www.rollingstone .com/music/news/beyonce-surprises-with-new-album -release-20131213.

35 Jocelyn Vena, "Beyoncé Reveals 'The Message' of Her New Album," *MTV News*, December 18, 2013, http://www.mtv.com /news/1719263/beyonce-album-message/.

35 Ann Oldenburg, "Beyoncé: 'Yes, I Am Powerful,'" *USA Today*, January 10, 2013, https://www.usatoday.com/story/life /people/2013/01/10/beyonce-yes-i-am-powerful/1822597/.

39 Toyin Owoseje, "Beyoncé Breaks Down in Tears as She Admits Fame Is a Burden in Short Film Yours and Mine," *International Business Times*, December 12, 2014, http://www.ibtimes.co.uk /beyonce-breaks-down-tears-she-admits-fame-burden-short -film-yours-mine-1479329.

SELECTED BIBLIOGRAPHY

Anderson, Trevor. "Rewinding the Charts: In 1999, Destiny's Child—and Beyoncé—Hit No. 1 for the First Time." *Billboard*, July 17, 2016. http://www.billboard.com/articles/columns/chart-beat/7439082 /rewinding-the-charts-in-1999-destinys-child-and-beyonce-hit-no-1.

Emery, Debbie. "No Awkward Phase Here! Beyoncé Looks Picture Perfect as a Glossy Young Teen in Her High School Yearbook." *Daily Mail. com*. Last modified May 29, 2013. http://www.dailymail.co.uk /tvshowbiz/article-2332151/Beyonce-picture-perfect-school-year -book-photos.html.

Hawgood, Alex. "The Matriarch behind Beyoncé and Solange." *New York Times*, January 21, 2017. https://www.nytimes.com/2017/01/21 /fashion/tina-knowles-lawson-beyonce-solange-matriarch.html.

Iandoli, Kathy. "A Complete Timeline of Beyoncé's Complicated Relationship with Her Father." *Cosmopolitan*, May 2, 2016. http://www.cosmopolitan.com/entertainment/celebs/a57822/beyonce -mathew-knowles-timeline/.

Lambe, Stacy. "Pre-Michelle: The Last Year the Original Destiny's Child Was Together." *VH1*, January 18, 2014. http://www.vh1.com /news/52365/original-destinys-child-last-year/.

Mancini, Rob. "Destiny's Child Sued by Former Members." *MTV News*, March 24, 2000. http://www.mtv.com/news/1428047/destinys-child -sued-by-former-members/.

FURTHER READING

BOOKS

Braun, Eric. *Prince: The Man, the Symbol, the Music.* Minneapolis: Lerner Publications, 2017. Music lovers will enjoy this biography of Prince, with whom Beyoncé shared the stage at the 2004 Grammy Awards.

Kampff, Joseph. *Beyoncé: Singer, Songwriter, and Actress.* New York: Enslow, 2016. Find out more about Beyoncé's life before and after she became a star.

——. *Jay-Z: Rapper and Businessman.* New York: Enslow, 2016. Learn how Beyoncé's husband transformed his life to become a powerful force in the music industry.

Kramer, Barbara. *Beyoncé: Singer, Songwriter, and Actress.* Minneapolis: Abdo, 2013. Splashy photos and interesting sidebars shed more light on the life of the queen of pop.

Krohn, Katherine. *Michael Jackson: Ultimate Music Legend.* Minneapolis: Lerner Publications, 2010. If Beyoncé' is the queen of pop, Michael Jackson is the king. Read all about him in this book.

Landau, Elaine. *Beyoncé: R & B Superstar.* Minneapolis: Lerner Publications, 2013. Learn more about the real Beyoncé Knowles and the struggles she faced becoming the superstar fans know and love.

Leigh, Anna. *Write and Record Your Own Songs.* Minneapolis: Lerner Publications, 2018. Dream of making it big in music like Beyoncé? Find out how to become a songwriter and share your art with new potential fans!

WEBSITES

Beyoncé

https://www.beyonce.com

On Beyoncé's official website, fans can stay up to date about her latest albums, tours, charity work, and more—including loads of pics!

Beyoncé: *Billboard*

https://www.billboard.com/music/beyonce

Get the latest news about Beyoncé and her music plus see where she lands on the charts.

Destiny's Child

http://www.DestinysChild.com

If you're looking for Destiny's Child music and videos, this site is the place. The band that launched Beyoncé's career stands the test of time.

INDEX